DECORATING T-SHIRTS

Ray Gibson
Edited by Paula Borton
Designed by Rebecca Halverson

Photographs by Ray Moller
Illustrated by Chris Chaisty
Series editor: Cheryl Evans

Models: Amanda Blainey; Eliza Borton; Jessica Borton; Joanna Borton; Jonathan Briscoe; Siaffa Bumduka; Laura Flowerdew; Harry Gibson; Dylan Green; Emma Lee; Chris Rasbash and Marina Townsend.

Additional T-shirt ideas: Non Figg; Rebecca Halverson; Rebecca Lilley; John Russell; Diane Thistlethwaite and Maria Wheatley.

Contents

Potato prints

Potato printing on T-shirts is great fun and easy to do. All you need is a potato and a few fabric paints to create some really bright, original prints. You will find that while some of your prints are bright and clear, others look blotchy and faded. Don't worry about this as these differences in shades and textures make them much more attractive than prints done by machines. For the fish, you need two potatoes; a craft or vegetable knife; a felt-tip pen; paintbrushes and fabric paints.

Print rows of reeds. Add a few on the sleeves.

Take care when cutting.

1. Draw the outline of a large fish with a felt-tip pen on one half of a prepared potato (see right). Cut carefully around the outline with a knife before cutting away the potato around the fish.

2. Do V-shaped cuts to make some markings on your fish (ask an adult to do this for you). Poke the end of a matchstick or the point of a ballpoint pen to mark an eye.

3. Blot the potato with kitchen towel to sop up any liquid. Paint the fish. Make sure the paint is evenly spread, but take care not to fill up the eyehole and stripes with paint.

You can make your fish look like the ones on this T-shirt by carving extra fins and markings on your potato before printing.

4. Prepare your T-shirt (see how on page 32). Do as many fish as you want. You don't have to repaint after each print as the fading paint gives an interesting texture.

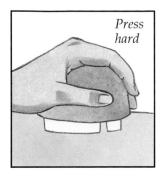

Press hard

5. In the same way as the fish, draw and cut reeds into a potato. Paint the reeds green and print them onto your T-shirt. Rock the potato slightly from side to side to get an even print.

6. Draw and cut a simple small fish to print as well. Turn the potato around to make the fish swim the other way. For bubbles, dip the end of a fat straw into paint and print.

Preparing potatoes

Choose potatoes about the same size and shape of the prints you want. Old potatoes are best for printing. Wash and dry the potatoes carefully, then cut them in half lengthwise and blot them with kitchen towel. Try leaving them in the refrigerator to dry out for two hours before cutting a design. This makes the job easier. When you have finished with your carved potato, wrap it up and put it in the refrigerator. It will keep for quite a few days.

Rainbow fish

Print bright rainbow fish by painting a potato in different shades. The paints should merge and blend slightly to give a rainbow effect. Make the fins and tail a really bright shade.

Skulls

Draw a simple skull shape onto half a potato. Now cut it out as shown in step 1 on page 2. Paint the skull black and print with it onto a really bright T-shirt. You could also try printing crossbones.

African prints

Carve out some African style designs from halved potatoes. Do a mask, some pots and some geometric shapes. Print them on a T-shirt using bronze, copper and black paints.

3

Executive shirt

Decorate a T-shirt with fabric crayons to transform yourself into a busy executive with a hectic day of meetings and conferences.

A long-sleeved T-shirt is good for this design as you can draw in cuffs.

You could do a striped or spotted tie.

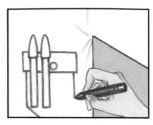

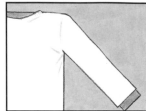

1. Prepare your T-shirt (see page 32). Gather up any loose fabric and tape it around the back. Put cardboard in the end of the sleeves.

2. With a black crayon, draw a pocket with pens, collar, tie and buttons. If you have a long-sleeved T-shirt, draw in some cuffs as well.

Always shade the same side.

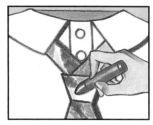

3. Shade along one side of the lines in black, then rub gently with your finger to get a smooth look. These shadows make the effect more realistic.

4. Iron the black to make it permanent. Follow the maker's instructions. The lines will not smudge now. Pattern the tie and do the pens. Iron again.

Tips

Fabric crayons can be tricky to use at first. Try them out on a scrap of material beforehand. If you find it difficult drawing the lines with the crayon you could use a black fabric pen instead.

You could first draw your design on the shirt using a soft pencil or pale chalk. Then go over it with a crayon.

Crocodile

This crocodile curls all the way around the back of the T-shirt. You will need a sponge about 14cm (5½in) long and 4cm (1½in) deep; some green, white, yellow and blue fabric paint; a black fabric pen and some extra sponge to print reeds. You can give your crocodile plastic wobbly eyes, if you like.

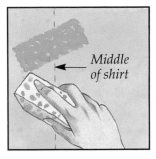

Middle of shirt

1. Spread green fabric paint on an old plate. Lightly dip a long side of the sponge into the paint and press two shapes onto the prepared T-shirt (see page 32), as shown.

Front of shirt

Tail

Dab on a foot.

2. Use a short end of the sponge to print shapes for the body. With a corner of the sponge dab on a foot and tip of a tail. The prints are outlined in black later on.

3. Draw nostrils, eyes and teeth in black. Paint the teeth white and the eyes yellow. Use scissors to cut some sponge into points for reeds and print them in blue.

4. When dry, turn the shirt over and continue printing the body to meet with the tail. Print a back foot and reeds. Draw a black wiggly line around the crocodile.

Make smaller prints near the tail.

Wobbly eyes

You can buy plastic wobbly eyes in dressmaking stores. If they have a prong at the back ask an adult to saw it off with a serrated knife. You also need squeeze-on paint (see page 32). Put a blob of paint on the back of the eye and press it on. Seal it by squeezing paint around the edges.

Doodles

There are lots of really good designs you can create with a few squeeze-on fabric paints. Try out your doodles on a piece of paper first or draw chalk outlines on the T-shirt for you to go over with paint.

Puff paint pig

You can buy paint which puffs up when heated. Follow the maker's directions. Avoid small designs as the paint spreads when puffed up. Try drawing a simple pig in pink.

Autographs

Ask all your friends to sign their names with a ballpoint pen on a T-shirt; make sure they do large, clear letters. Go over them with bright paint.

Hearts

Rows of small objects like these hearts look really effective.

Frog

Draw the outline of a large, cartoon frog. Use green squeeze-on paint.

Bee

Draw on a wicked-looking bee. Do a winding trail to show its flight path.

Draw on the back view of the pig (above right) to add a comic touch to your T-shirt.

Stick man

Cut an oblong shape out of cardboard. Use this as a stencil to sponge a panel background for a stick man (see page 9 for more help with stencils).

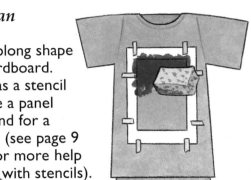

Blackboard

This jokey design needs only white paint and a black T-shirt. Write or draw anything you please on your blackboard. Don't forget to do the back as well.

Do stick men in all sorts of poses. See right for more stick men ideas.

Write lots of numbers and spellings on your blackboard.

Tip

If you make a mistake with the squeeze-on paint, scrape it off with a blunt knife and start again.

More stick people

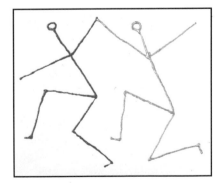

You could design a "whiteboard" by drawing black on a white T-shirt.

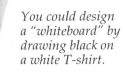

Monster foot

Make your own stencil for this jokey monster foot. This stencil is very simple, but you can make more complicated ones with lots of "bridges". The bridges are the strips of cardboard separating the cut-out areas. The bridges on this stencil are in between the toes. If you cut these by mistake, just patch them with tape on both sides.

   For the monster foot you will need some cardboard, scissors and tape, as well as some green and yellow fabric paint.

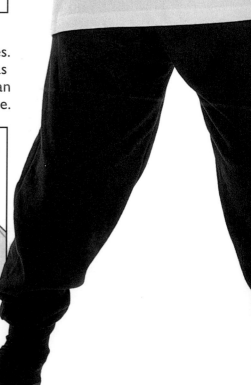

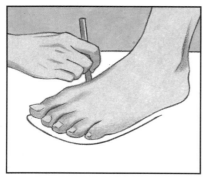

1. On a big piece of cardboard draw around a large foot (ask your dad or a large friend to stand on the cardboard). Don't draw between the toes.

2. Once you have your main shape, draw on some big toes. You can give your monster as many toes as you like, you can also make them a funny shape.

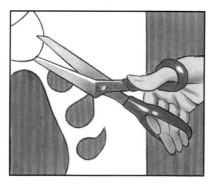

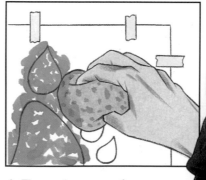

3. With a pencil point, poke a hole in the main foot shape, then push the scissors through the hole to cut out the shape. Do the same with the toes.

4. Tape the stencil onto your prepared T-shirt (see page 32). Sponge on green paint (see tips), then add some yellow.

Bat and moon

It doesn't matter if the paint is a bit patchy.

These bats are made with a reverse stencil. This means that a pattern is created by painting the outer area around a stencil. Remember that your design will be the same shade as your T-shirt.

The bat stencils are made from sticky-backed plastic*. You also need silver paint, tape, a rag and cardboard.

Make some smaller bats to fly around the moon.

Stencil tips

Ordinary cardboard is fine for making stencils, although in stationers' you can buy special stencilling card. Sticky-backed plastic* makes excellent T-shirt stencils as its stickiness means the stencil won't shift while you are painting. It is specially good if you want sharp lines on the design (see Bat and moon). It's best to dab paint on the stencil area with a sponge or rag. Spread the paint on an old saucer. Don't lift the stencil until the paint is dry.

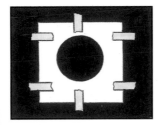

1. Draw and cut out a circle from cardboard (draw around a large plate). Tape this moon-shaped stencil onto your T-shirt.

2. Fold a piece of paper and then with a pencil draw half a bat on the fold. Cut it out through both layers of paper.

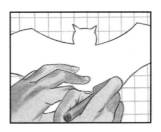

3. Open out the bat and lay it on the back of the plastic. Draw around the shape and cut it out. Peel off the backing.

4. Stick the bat inside the moon. Dab silver all over with a crumpled rag. When dry, remove the cardboard and the bat.

9

* contact paper U.S

Comic blow-up

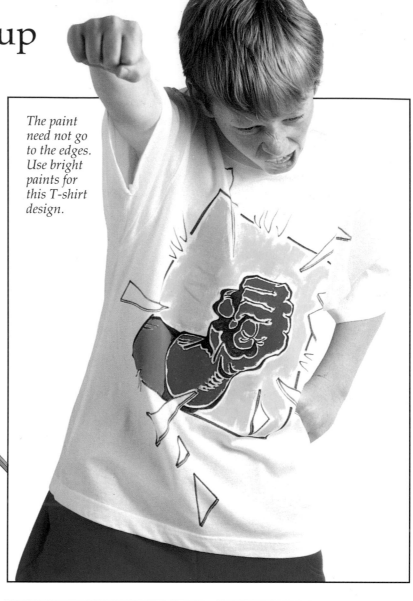

You can blow up a design or picture you like so that it is big enough to copy onto a T-shirt. This technique is called "squaring up". Look at page 30 for the comic book style designs shown on these T-shirts.

You need greaseproof paper, carbon paper, fabric paints, paintbrushes, tape and a black fabric pen.

The paint need not go to the edges. Use bright paints for this T-shirt design.

Fist

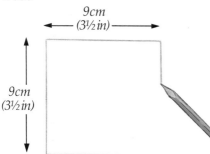

9cm (3½ in)

9cm (3½ in)

1. Measure the fist picture on page 30. Draw a square the same size onto the middle of a big sheet of greaseproof paper.

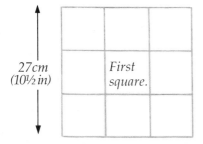

27cm (10½ in)

First square.

2. Add a square the same size either side, and three squares above and three below. The outline is now three times bigger than the first square.

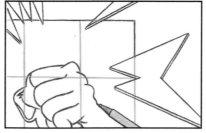

3. Copy what you see in each square in the book onto your grid (squares on the paper). Draw the shapes around the edge with a ruler.

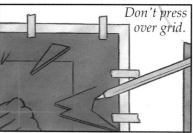

Don't press over grid.

4. Tape sheets of carbon ink-side-down to the prepared shirt (see page 32). Tape the drawing on top. Press over the picture with a ballpoint pen.

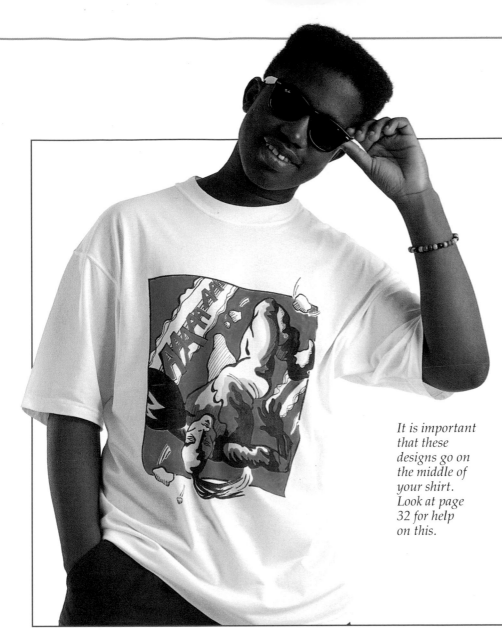

It is important that these designs go on the middle of your shirt. Look at page 32 for help on this.

"AAAAA!"

This dynamic scene looks really spectacular on a white T-shirt. You can do this design in exactly the same way as "Fist". You will find the picture to copy on page 31.

You can use any shades of paint you like, but reds, oranges and yellows show up very brightly and give the right comic strip feel to your design. It doesn't matter if the paint does not go right to the edges or if there are a few white gaps.

5. Lift off the tracing and carbon paper to see the copied picture. Go over all the lines with black pen. Use a ruler for the glass shapes.

6. Now paint the picture. Don't forget to add black shadows on the fist. It doesn't matter if the paint is patchy; this adds to the comic book effect.

Squaring up

Blow up any pictures you like using this technique. Draw a square around the image on tracing paper. Draw a grid of squares within this outline like the ones printed on the "Fist" and "AAAAA" pictures. Blow up the picture by following the steps here.

11

Glow-in-the-dark skull

Glow-in the-dark fabric paints look really good on black T-shirts. Wear your skull and crossbones in a darkened room and they will shine eerily.

Glow-in-the-dark or neon fabric paints can be easily bought and usually come in small, plastic bottles. Use a piece of white chalk or dressmakers' chalk to make an outline you can go over with the paint.

1. Draw a large skull in chalk onto your prepared shirt. You can dust off the chalk and start again if you want to change anything.

2. When you have done the skull, draw the crossbones underneath, like this. Add some sparks around the skull for a dramatic effect.

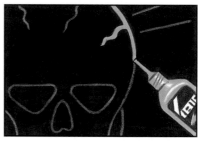

3. When you are happy with your design, squeeze a line of paint around it. It's a good idea to have a practice on a piece of scrap material first.

4. Change the paint as you go, for a really startling effect. Let the paints merge where they join. Allow the paint to dry completely.

You can copy the shape of this skull.

More glowing ideas

Draw lots of spooky eyes on your T-shirt. They will shine out in the dark.

Draw stars, moons and meteors all over your leggings as well as your T-shirt to make a complete outfit.

A glow-in-the-dark space scene looks really good on a black T-shirt.

Try drawing a picture of a friendly sea monster or a fiery dragon.

A cobweb is simple to do. You could add in your own scary spider.

Tip

Never iron over this paint as it will melt. To iron the shirt, turn it inside out and iron it under a damp cloth on a gentle heat.

Splash and splatter

These zany T-shirts are fun to do and completely original as you can never make two the same. For the rainbow print on this page, you will need bright paints and plastic food wrap. For the splatter shirt on the page opposite, you need a large paintbrush and fabric paints.

Shirt must be flat at the front.

1. Prepare your shirt (see page 32). Wrap the sleeves and any other parts you don't want painted around the back and tape.

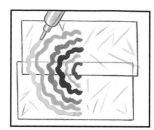

2. Cut two pieces of food wrap and join them by overlapping one long side of each. Squirt paint in half circles on one side.

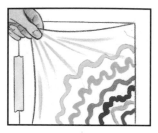

3. Tape the edge of the painted side to the surface to stop it from slipping. Fold the unpainted side of the food wrap on top.

4. With your fingers, push the paint toward the edges to get a sunburst effect. Then unpeel the top layer to find a circle pattern.

5. Take your T-shirt and press it firmly onto the paint. Then carefully lift it off. Fix the paint, if you need to, when dry.

The splashes should erupt all around the central splodge.

The paints will mix slightly. If you don't want this effect then let each one dry before flicking another.

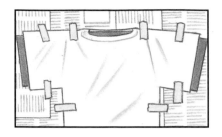

1. Prepare your T-shirt (see page 32). If you can't do this design out of doors, then protect your surroundings from splashes (see Tip). Put cardboard backing in the arms.

2. Water the paints down slightly but don't make them too runny as they lose their brightness. Also, if they are too runny they will drip off the brush.

Spatter patterns

You can make really good patterns by sticking on different shapes before spattering paint. For this shirt cut an oblong shape out of a big piece of cardboard. Now lay this over the prepared T-shirt (see page 32) so that the shirt is all covered apart from the oblong shape. Put some gummed stars, strips of tape and so on onto the shirt.

Dip a toothbrush into black paint then draw a blunt knife over the bristles toward you. The paint will flick onto the shirt. When dry, lift off the cardboard and peel off all the sticky paper.

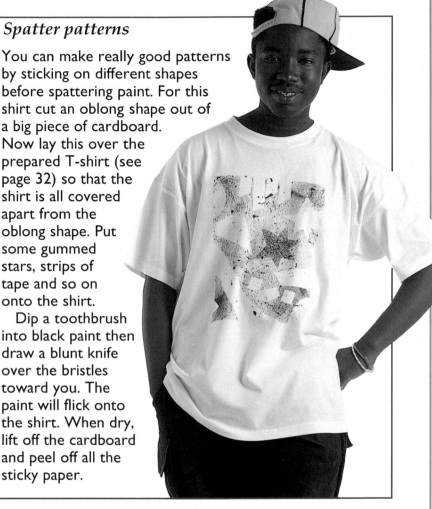

3. Starting with blue, paint a splodge in the middle of the shirt. Then still using blue, flick paint at the splodge so that splashes spurt out from the middle.

4. Flick a different shade of paint, still aiming at the middle. Do the same with a few other paints, but don't use too many as it will look messy. Let the paint dry.

Tip
If you want to splatter indoors cut a side of a large box and open it up. Lay the T-shirt inside.

Shells

You can stick all sorts of shapes and patterns onto your T-shirt using bonding fabric. This can be bought in dressmakers' stores. You also need some light cotton material in a shade that will go with your T-shirt, squeeze-on glitter fabric paint, tracing paper and carbon paper. You don't need to wash new shirts before decorating them in this way.

You can make up shell shapes of your own.

Ask an adult to do this.

1. Iron the bonding fabric to the wrong side of the cotton, following the instructions which come with the fabric.

2. Trace the shells on page 30. Put the carbon paper, ink-side-down, onto the right side of the cotton.

Do snails and leaves in the same way, but draw them straight onto the cotton after you have ironed on the bonding fabric.

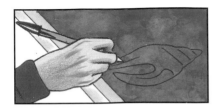

3. Lay the tracing on the carbon paper. Press over the outline with a ballpoint pen. Trace out a number of shells.

4. Lift the tracing and carbon paper. Cut out the shells. Peel off the backing and arrange the shells on the T-shirt.

5. Iron the shapes onto your shirt. Add shells to the back, in the same way. Prepare your shirt for painting (see page 32).

6. Go around the edges and carbon lines with glitter paint. Let the paint dry before doing the back.

Soccer player

You could wear one of your own works of art, like this soccer sketch. Iron bonding fabric to white cotton and draw a design with fabric pens or paints. Cut it out and bond it onto a T-shirt (see steps 4 and 5).

Stripes and numbers

Make your own team shirt by sticking a number or your initials onto a T-shirt. Iron bonding fabric onto some light cotton material and then draw and cut out numbers. Bond them to your shirt as in steps 4 and 5.

Dinosaur

The technique used here is very much like batik, but instead of hot wax you use a flour and water paste to "resist" the paint.

You will need yellow, orange, red and black fabric paints, flour and cardboard to make a stencil.

You could draw your own dinosaur onto tracing paper and then copy it onto your T-shirt using carbon paper (see Tiger on page 22 for help).

1. Draw and cut out a dinosaur stencil (see right) and tape it onto your prepared T-shirt (see page 32). Sponge on yellow, orange and red and let it dry.

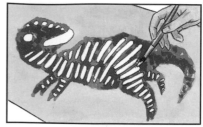

2. Mix flour and water to a thick creamy paste. Dip a small paintbrush in the paste and paint an eye, mouth and markings. The pasted parts on your dinosaur will later show up really brightly.

The stencil

Draw a rectangle on cardboard as big as you want your dinosaur. Make it half as wide as it is long, so if it is 44cm (18in) long, make it 22cm (9in) wide. Divide the rectangle into 4, then 8 and 16. Copy the pictures on the right from square to square. Do humps on the back. Cut out to make the stencil.

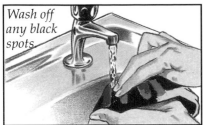
Wash off any black spots

Tip

If the paste becomes gluey, mix a fresh batch or it will drag the fabric as you paint.

3. Let the paste dry. Paint black over the dinosaur, using a fine brush to do the edges. Let it dry. If the paint needs to be heat fixed, lay the shirt on a sheet of paper and iron the design on the wrong side.

4. Soak the shirt in cold water for a few minutes. Peel off the paste under a tap. When dry, paint teeth and eye middles black.

Psychedelic patterns

1. Prepare the T-shirt (see page 32), then pencil on a circle. You could draw around a round tray. Dab on bright paints using a brush or sponge.

2. Let the paint dry and brush on patterns with a flour paste as in step 2. Try swirly patterns. Paint on black as described in step 3 above.

3. Follow step 4 above to finish off the design. Try and experiment with other shapes and designs. You could do a spiral pattern as shown here.

Brick wall

Print a brick wall on a T-shirt, then scrawl on your own graffiti. You can also print bricks just halfway up a T-shirt, then stencil on a black cat, some gold stars and a moon. Turn to page 9 for advice on stencilling.

For a brick wall T-shirt, you need some tape (masking tape is best for this) and red, brown and black fabric paint.

If you print bricks on the back, make sure they line up with the front ones.

The cat, moon and stars are simple stencils to make (see page 9 for help).

The plate keeps the neckband clean.

1. Tape a small plate over the neck of your prepared T-shirt (see page 32). Then put some pieces of cardboard inside the sleeves.

2. Tape along the bottom of the shirt. Cut two cardboard brick shapes 20cm x 9cm (8in x 3½in). Line up the bricks on the top edge of the tape.

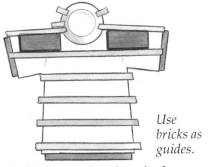

Use bricks as guides.

3. Stick another band of tape across, just above the bricks. Do this all the way up the shirt so that it is evenly striped with tape.

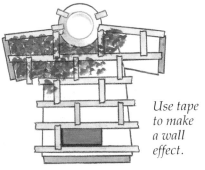

Use tape to make a wall effect.

4. Add strips of tape going the other way. Use the length of a brick as a guide. Mix red and brown paint and dab it over the shirt with a sponge.

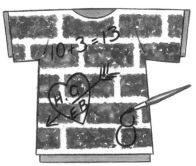

5. When dry, unpeel the tape and take off the plate. Now do the back of the shirt in the same way. When all the paint is dry, add graffiti in black.

Bright blocks

This stylish design can be created with strips of masking tape, a sponge and some paint. Stick four strips of tape to form a square in the middle of your T-shirt. Put more strips both across and down within the square to form a grid pattern. Keep the strips about 2½cm (1in) apart. Sponge paint in the spaces between the tape. Start with a light shade.

Starry stripes

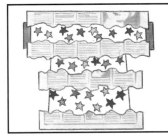

1. Tear a wavy strip from eight layers of newspaper and pin on four of the strips. Put gummed stars on the uncovered parts.

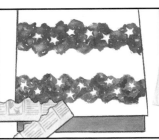

2. Sponge paint over the starred areas. When dry, take off the paper and stars. Do the back with the four leftover strips.

Match up the front and back stripes.

Tiger and cheetah

These dramatic animal heads are easy to do. For the tiger, you need red, yellow, green and black paint; tape; some sheets of carbon and tracing paper and a black fabric pen. A white T-shirt makes a good background for the tiger.

Tiger

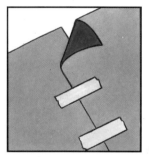

Tape the non-ink side.

1. Trace the half template on page 31 (you can see how to do it on the same page). Now tape sheets of carbon paper to make a piece big enough to cover the tracing.

Don't forget to paint in whiskers.

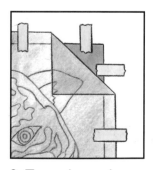

See page 32 for how to find the middle.

2. Tape the carbon paper, ink-side-down, onto your prepared T-shirt (see page 32). Tape the tracing on top, matching its fold line with the middle of the T-shirt.

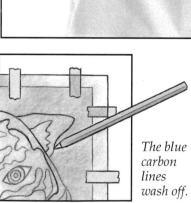

The blue carbon lines wash off.

3. Go over all the lines on the tracing with a ballpoint pen, pressing firmly. Take off the tracing and carbon and you will find the outline has copied onto the shirt in blue.

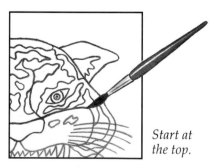

Start at the top.

4. With a very thin paintbrush or a black fabric pen go over the outline. You could rest your hand on a clean piece of paper so the carbon lines don't get smudged.

22

Don't worry if the carbon lines show up after you've finished painting, these will come off when the T-shirt is washed.

Cheetah

Paint a cheetah using the outline of the same template. Use a light brown T-shirt for the fur and then paint in black markings, following the picture below. Once dry, paint in the white, brown and red parts. Do two coats of white. See page 32 for the best paint to use.

Go over outline again, if too faint.

5. Fill in the black areas (use the template and photograph as painting guides). You might need to do two coats of black to prevent the fabric from showing through.

6. When the black is dry, paint the rest of the face. You will need to mix the paints for some areas. Once dry, follow the maker's instructions for fixing the paints.

Tips

When you use carbon paper, the ink can stain your hands. If you don't want inky smudges on your T-shirt, remember to wash your hands before touching it.

You could try painting the head of another of the big cats. Use the basic outline of the template on page 31 and paint in different markings. Look at wildlife books for more ideas.

Around the world

All the designs here are inspired by different parts of the world. There is an African mask, an Aboriginal crocodile from Australia and an Aztec print from South America. The mask and the crocodile are done with simple stencils that you make yourself. The mask stencil is easy to draw as it is made up of very simple shapes. You can copy the picture on step 1. Look at page 9 for help with stencils.
For the mask you will need tracing and carbon paper; brown and black paints; cardboard; tape and gummed round labels.

You can make the mask as big or small as you like. You could do some potato prints around the sleeve (see pages 2-3).

African mask

This makes sure both sides are equal.

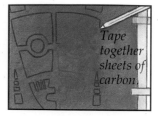

Tape together sheets of carbon.

1. Fold a big sheet of greaseproof or tracing paper. Draw half the mask. Turn the paper over and go over the lines showing through.

2. Tape carbon paper, ink-side-down onto cardboard. Tape the tracing onto the carbon and go over the lines with a ballpoint pen.

3. Take off the tracing and carbon paper. Cut out the stencil. You could use a craft knife but be careful as they are very sharp.

4. Tape the stencil on the prepared T-shirt (see page 32). Stick a label on each eye and sponge on paint. When dry, lift off the stencil.

Aboriginal crocodile

1. Draw a simple crocodile shape and cut it out. Don't worry if the crocodile isn't very realistic.

2. Lay the stencil on the shirt. Sponge on black paint. When dry, lift the stencil. Fix the paint, if you need to.

Aztec potato prints

You can copy these pictures.

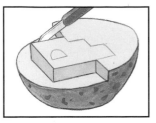

1. Prepare potatoes as described on page 3. Draw each design on a potato. Cut the potatoes as in step 1 on page 2.

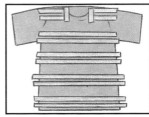

2. Put two strips of tape ½cm (¼in) apart above the T-shirt hem. Do this five times. Leave equal gaps between.

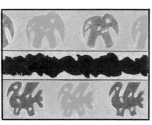

3. Potato print between each double row of tape. Sponge black in the narrow tape gaps. When dry peel off the tape.

Decorate around the crocodile with squiggles and dots.

If you make a mistake, scrape off paint with a blunt knife.

Print a black line on the sleeves.

3. Outline the crocodile with white squeeze-on paint. Don't forget teeth and eyes. Use red on the body.

Poppy

You need bright red, green and black paint, tape and a sheet of newspaper for this really striking design.

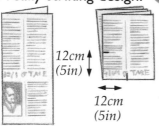

1. Fold a sheet of newspaper into four and then from the inner corner measure 12cm (5in) along each side and mark, as shown.

2. Draw an uneven shape, like the top of a heart, using the marks as guides. Then tear it out. Don't use scissors as the edges need to be rough.

3. Open out the paper stencil and tape it onto your prepared T-shirt (see page 32). Sponge on red paint (see page 9 for help on stencils).

4. When the red is dry, paint on a black middle. Add black lines for stamens; squeeze-on paint is good for this. Paint on a green stem and leaf.

Tip

If you don't like your torn shape try again with another sheet of paper. Check to see if the stencil will fit on your shirt. Tear a bigger or smaller poppy shape according to the size of your T-shirt.

Daisy

You need a large sheet of cardboard and some bright fabric paints for this big daisy.

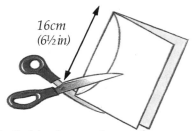

16cm
(6½in)

1. Fold a large piece of paper. Draw half a petal shape about 16cm (6½in) long on the fold. Cut it out through both layers of paper.

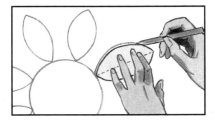

2. Place a saucer in the middle of the cardboard and pencil around it. Draw petals around the rim of the circle, using the cut-out petal as a guide.

Make the size of the petals and the inner circle smaller if you want to decorate a small size T-shirt.

You could make a stencil for the middle of the flower if you want a perfect circle.

3. Poke a hole in one of the drawn petals and push the blade of your scissors through to cut out the shape. Do the same with all the petals.

4. Lay the stencil onto your prepared T-shirt (see page 32). Sponge paint onto all the petals (see page 9 for more stencilling tips).

5. When the petals are dry, lift off the cardboard. Sponge a circle of paint onto the middle. When dry, dot squeeze-on paint for a raised effect.

Even more T-shirt ideas

On this double page there are more T-shirt designs to inspire you, many of them using the techniques described earlier in the book.

Stick on stars and a moon (see page 9) and sponge gold or silver around them. Spatter on more paint for a starry sky effect.

Trace the outline of the tiger template on page 31. Also trace the eyes and nose. See page 22 for how to copy it onto your T-shirt. Draw in a mane and paint brown for a lion.

You can make interesting prints with everyday objects (below left). A plastic fork; toothbrush; a sponge and string have been used here. Can you spot what other things were used?

For this mottled effect dampen the shirt and wrinkle into tiny pleats (the shirt ends up sausage shaped). Drip on paint with an eye-dropper and open out.

The design below has been made by cutting pictures out of a fabric and then sticking them onto a T-shirt with bonding fabric.

Use the flour and water paste technique on pages 18-19 to create this African mask.

This geometric pattern above, has been made with potato prints. See pages 2-3 for how to print with potatoes.

Draw on a simple face with squeeze-on paint (left).

Use fabric crayons for the bright tropical scene in the middle (see page 4).

29

Templates

On these pages you will find the templates (outline shapes) for the Tiger (page 22) and the Shell T-shirt (page 16). The designs for the Comic blow-ups (pages 10-11) are also here.

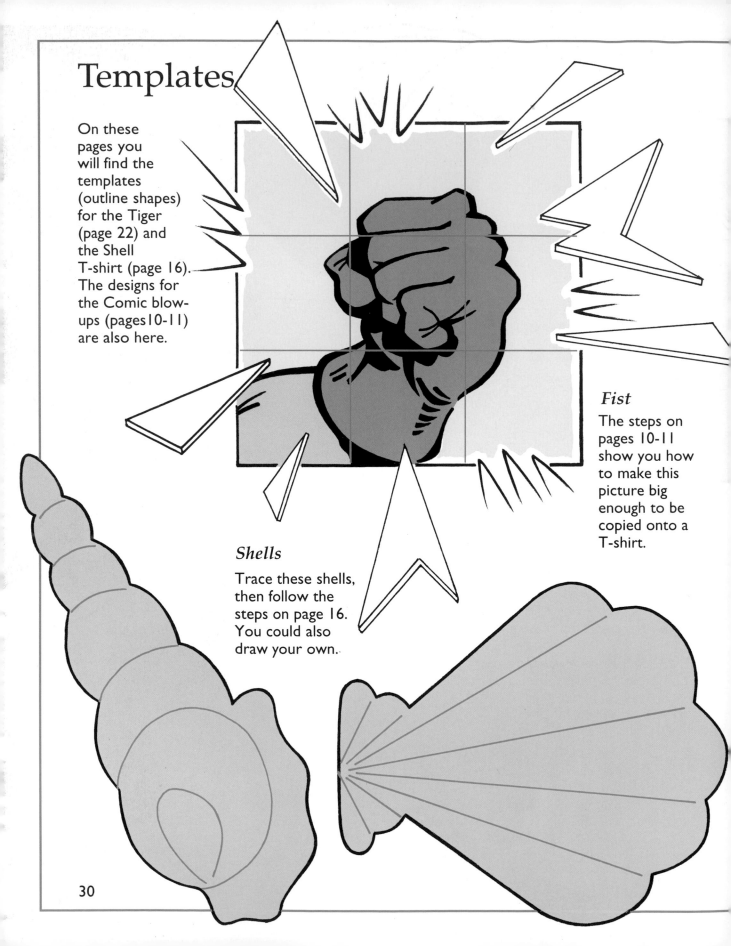

Fist

The steps on pages 10-11 show you how to make this picture big enough to be copied onto a T-shirt.

Shells

Trace these shells, then follow the steps on page 16. You could also draw your own.

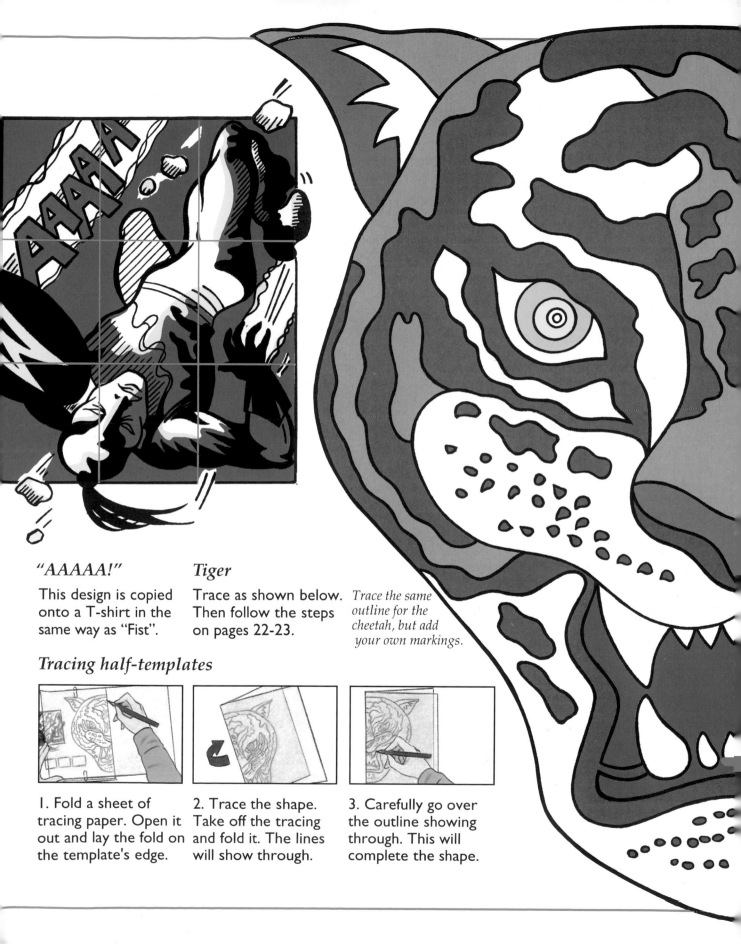

"AAAAA!"

This design is copied onto a T-shirt in the same way as "Fist".

Tiger

Trace as shown below. Then follow the steps on pages 22-23.

Trace the same outline for the cheetah, but add your own markings.

Tracing half-templates

1. Fold a sheet of tracing paper. Open it out and lay the fold on the template's edge.

2. Trace the shape. Take off the tracing and fold it. The lines will show through.

3. Carefully go over the outline showing through. This will complete the shape.

T-shirt know-how

T-shirts

It is great fun and very satisfying to decorate your own T-shirts; it also doesn't have to cost you a lot of money. Old T-shirts are good for decorating, especially if you just want to try out a new design. If you are buying a new T-shirt, remember that good cotton T-shirts are best for painting. Try and have some scraps of material at hand to experiment on.

Finding the middle

Front of T-shirt

For many designs in this book you need to mark the middle of the shirt. Fold the ironed shirt, matching the sleeves. Mark the middle with a pin at the top and bottom of the fold.

Preparing T-shirts

If you are using a new T-shirt, you need to wash it before painting. Most new clothes have a "dressing" which must be washed out if the paint is to be properly absorbed into the material. You also need to iron your T-shirt before painting. If you are using a non-white shirt, test paint on the inside hem as, for instance, yellow on a blue T-shirt may end up as green.

You need to put some backing inside the shirt to stop the paint from seeping through. Some cardboard covered with foil will do. Try and find a piece of cardboard about 1cm (½in) wider than your T-shirt so that the fabric is lightly stretched. Cover all work surfaces. Tape the shirt edges down to keep it flat. Leave the cardboard inside until the paint is dry to prevent smudging.

Fabric paints

You need to think about your T-shirt design before buying any fabric paints, as the paints can vary in the sorts of effects they create. You don't have to spend a lot of money on paints, as often you only need a couple to make a really effective design. You can buy the paints very easily in art and hobby stores and stationers'.

Many of the fabric paints need to be "fixed", (made permanent and washable) which is usually done by ironing your finished design. It is best to ask an adult to do this. Remember to read the directions on the paints before you start, as the methods to "fix" the paint can vary from brand to brand. You can use different types of paint on one design, but remember they may need to be treated in different ways.

Liquid acrylic paint is excellent for T-shirt painting. It can be watered down and does not need to be fixed to make it permanent. It brushes on smoothly and so is good for painting large areas, such as the Tiger (page 22) . "Liquitex" is a well-known brand of this paint.

Ordinary fabric paints. There is a huge variety to choose from. They usually have to be fixed by ironing. Some paints are thicker than others, but you can also buy small tubes of paint which water down well. Dylon, Deka and Delta are brand names of these fabric paints.

Fabric crayons. Try not to attempt shading large areas with these as it can be hard work.

Fabric pens are good for writing and outlining designs on T-shirts.

Squeeze-on fabric paints (dimensional paints) come in small plastic bottles. They give a raised outline or pattern. It is a good idea to try out the paint on a scrap of fabric before you start. You can also buy paint like this which glows in the dark (see page 12) as well as glitter and puff paint.